# 1
## BLACK HOLE PATROL

"LOOK, NUMBSKULL!" barked Roberta. "Don't ask what I'll do for you as class prefect – it's what I'll do to you if you don't vote for me! I'll introduce a special VAT – Very Aggressive Tax – on anyone who has the nerve to oppose me."

She swept out of the classroom like a rhino that's been laser-zapped in a tender spot.

"Phewww...!!" said Ben in the silence that followed. "Is life at this school always as bad as this?"

*Also available in Lions*

Samson Superslug   *Ken Adams*
Survival Guide to Parents   *Scoular Anderson*
Ellie Scrimshaw and the Hounds of Gobbolot
*Dick Cate*

**The Black Hole series by
Brough Girling / Damian Kelleher**

Dead Rat Birthday Cake
A Spot of Bother
The Reign of Terror

Survival Guide to School *Brough Girling*
My Babysitter is a Vampire   *Ann Hodgman*
The Third Class Genie   *Robert Leeson*

# BLACK HOLE PATROL

## Brough Girling and Damian Kelleher

### Illustrated by
### Robin Edmonds

Lions
*An Imprint of HarperCollinsPublishers*

First published in Great Britain in Lions in 1994
3 5 7 9 10 8 6 4 2

Lions is an imprint of HarperCollins Children's Books,
a division of HarperCollins Publishers Ltd,
77-85 Fulham Palace Road, Hammersmith,
London W6 8JB

Text copyright © 1994  Brough Girling and
Damian Kelleher
Illustrations copyright © 1994 Robin Edmonds

ISBN 0 00 674711 6

The authors assert their moral right to be
identified as the authors of the work.

Printed and bound in Great Britain
by HarperCollins Manufacturing Ltd, Glasgow

# CHAPTER ONE

"Ben! Ben! I'm not going to call you again. If you're not down here in five minutes you'll be extremely sorry."

Ben's mother's voice blasted out from the voice transmitter just above Ben's pillow. He turned over in bed and yawned. Oh well, he knew when he was beaten. Better get ready for school, he thought.

On an ordinary day, Ben wouldn't have minded getting on to his solar-charged scooter and zapping off to Milky Way Juniors. But this wasn't an ordinary day. Ben and his mum had just moved twenty thousand light kilometres west of Jupiter to Stratus B, right on the edge of the universe. "Black Hole country", the locals called it, on account of the huge gaping mass that dominated the whole area, the biggest, suckiest, blackest black hole

5

yet discovered in the cosmos.

Today was a big day for Ben Gordon and his mother. Mrs Gordon started her new job as a Black Hole Patrol Warden. And Ben started his new school very reluctantly.

Ben padded out of his room across the temperature-regulated floor and stepped into the shower cubicle. Selecting auto-wash one (not too vigorous for first thing in the morning, unlike auto-wash two or three, for example, which nearly took your head off) he also pressed the shampoo button (problem hair – frequent wash) and thought a moment while his finger hovered over the conditioner switch.

Oh, why not, he thought. A dude has to look his best for the first day at a new school, after all, even if it was The School That Time Forgot.

Mrs Gordon was sitting at the kitchen table leafing nervously through the *Galaxy Gazette*.

"Just look at the time, Ben," she scolded her eleven-year-old son. "You'll make me late for my first day on patrol, you will. Whatever will the other wardens think of me? I've waited two years to get a decent job like this. Heaven knows, since your father dematerialised we need the money. So come on, shake a leg. Get your Puffed Planets down you or we'll be here all day."

Oh-oh, thought Ben. First day nerves. He pressed a key on a sensor pad on the table and Herbie, the home robot, powered over to the table with a box of Puffed Planets on a tray. Herbie was a little erratic at times. Sometimes it was easier to do things for yourself, even though he'd had an overhaul the week before last to iron out all his systems errors.

Ben poured the neon green cereal into a bowl laid out for him on the foil tablecloth. There in the middle of the heap sat what

looked suspiciously like a maroon 1994 model Ford Fiesta.

"What have you got there?" His mother peered at him over the top of her paper.

Ben held the small car up to the light. "Another Ford Fiesta," he sighed. "That's the fifth one now. I'm not collecting these vintage cars any more," he moaned. "I don't even like Puffed Planets."

"That's the trouble with you, Ben," his mother said sternly. "You're too impatient by half. What is it you need now?"

Ben had a sort of sulky look on his face. He was tall for his age, with sandy-coloured hair and just the right amount of freckles like a sprinkling of chocolate drops across his nose. He wasn't bad looking really when he wasn't screwing his face up in a sulk, like now.

"I've told you, Mum. All I need for the set is an Austin Allegro. I don't believe they've made any. It's a con."

Mrs Gordon jumped up in a flurry. She often made rapid movements that tended to startle other people. "Well, take the silly thing to school with you. You might be able to do a swap with someone. You never know. You might make a new friend."

Friends. Don't talk to me about friends, thought Ben. He'd left his best friend Krishnan behind at Milky Way Junior. Ben made a mental note to call him later on the tele-speaker and check if he'd got the Austin Allegro yet.

"Look at the time!" Mrs Gordon was acting like a mini-whirlwind now, rushing about the table, picking things up and elbowing Herbie from the sink. "Haven't you finished yet?" She didn't even wait for an answer. "Now where's my silly cap?"

She picked the jaunty peaked number off the floor and arranged it carefully on her mass of fluffy brown curls. Twirling round majestically in her navy uniform with a powder pink stripe, she put a mean traffic warden look on her face.

"Well, will I do? Am I the belle of the patrol or am I the belle of the patrol?"

"You look stupid," said Ben. "You don't look tough at all. Can't you be a bit more Robocop-ish? You wouldn't scare me into keeping away from a black hole."

Ben's mother pushed him roughly towards the door.

"We'll see. *I* may not scare you, my lad," she warned. "But just wait till you see your new headmaster. He'll blow your bloomin' socks off!"

# CHAPTER TWO

Ben had always quite enjoyed assembly at Milky Way Junior. Miss Jenkinson would breeze into the hall with a bright smile on her bright green face (she was a Dacron, from the galaxy Dac, who are happy-go-lucky sorts), then they'd sing a few songs and get on with their day. You knew where you were at Milky Way.

Ben didn't know where he was at Black Hole Primary.

He arrived in the large entrance chamber much too early, for which of course he blamed his mum. He stood around like a robot with a flat battery until a laser siren went off and a school secretary came out of her office. "Can I help you, young man?" she asked.

"I'm new here," said Ben. "I'm Ben Gordon."

11

"Ah, yes. Hello Ben. You'll be in Pulsar Remove. I'm Mrs McTavish, the school secretary." The kind-looking lady gave him a smile and a wink.

"Cheer up," she said. "The first day is always the worst, you know. Now it's assembly in a minute. I suggest you go down to the hall, right down the corridor, first turning on your left."

Not much later Ben was standing in one of several rows, in the Back Hole school hall. It was large and noisy and filled with children, and Ben didn't know if he had the courage to speak to anyone.

On his left was a boy, a black Earthling, taller than Ben. On the other side was a Martian girl who was speaking in a loud, bossy voice to kids in the row in front: "Just hand over the pocket money," she hissed, "and forget the excuses. Just you wait till I'm form prefect. You lot won't know what's hit you!"

Suddenly Mrs McTavish, the friendly school secretary, walked on to the large stage. "Quiet, Black Hole Primary, please! Assembly beginning." She had to shout above the din.

As a hush fell, the tall boy next to Ben

put his hand in front of his mouth and whispered to him: "Say, man, you new here?"

"Yeah," whispered back Ben.

"Wait till you see the Head. He'll freak you out!"

Teachers had now arrived on the stage and were in rows facing the children. Ben had no time to examine them before there was a shuffling behind some curtains and suddenly a brightly dressed woman appeared pushing what Ben first took to be a rather elaborate supermarket trolley. She parked the trolley at the front of the stage.

"Good morning children!" she said loudly. Ben saw that her mouth was as red and almost as big as the hole in a letterbox.

"GOODMORNINGMISSWAGSTAFF," said the children all round. But Ben was

13

concentrating on the supermarket trolley.

It wasn't a supermarket trolley at all. It was a high-tech affair, with what was obviously some kind of power unit on the bottom shelf, and lots of wires and pipes leading up to the top of it. They seemed to be connected to a large glass dome, and it was the contents of the glass dome that took Ben's breath away.

GOOG MORNING PUPIPS...

It looked a bit like a huge uncooked egg, except that it was grey in colour and appeared to have a large glob of white jelly on the top which looked horribly as if it might be some kind of eye. Ben could see that from time to time it moved. Was the whole thing some kind of brain? Ben had never seen anything so revolting in his life – including school dinners.

"Silence please, children. For those of you who joined us for the first time today, I'm Miss Wagstaff, the Deputy Head," said the woman in the brightly coloured clothes. "Now the Head would like to say a few words."

There was a loud crackle from a small speaker which Ben could now clearly see on the front of the trolley's power pack:

"GOOG MORNING CHILDREN... AND WELCOMET TO ALL NEW PUPIPS TO BLACK HOLE PRIMARY..."

The voice was loud and echoey. Ben could hardly believe his ears – or his eyes.

"I'M THE HEAD. I'M SHSHORE YOU'LL BE VERY HAPPIP HERE – ESPECIALOID WHEN YOU GET USHED TO OUR LITTLE WAYS..."

The speaker crackled back into silence, and Miss Wagstaff stepped forward and made some announcements. Ben didn't listen to any of them. He couldn't take his eyes off the eye on top of the Head in the glass jar. It swivelled around like a hideous sea creature looking for food.

Trust my mum, he said to himself as the children turned and started filing out of the hall... Trust her to send me to a school where the Head is a brain in a bottle, and the Deputy's got a gob like a letterbox...

"Hey man!" said the black boy with a grin. "Call me Vernon and give me five!" He held out a large flat palm that Ben slapped gently with a downward movement. "It ain't so bad here," said Vernon, as if reading Ben's thoughts. "Stick with me and I'll show you round – like a cookie!" Vernon gave Ben a huge beaming broad grin.

"Thanks," said Ben. "I'm Ben."

"Say..." said Vernon, "you might be able to help me, Ben." He started to fumble with one hand in the pocket of his jacket. "You wouldn't happen to have a 1994 Ford Fiesta, would you?"

Vernon held out something in his long-fingered hand towards Ben. Ben instantly recognised it. A plastic Austin Allegro.

# CHAPTER THREE

"What class you in, dude?" Vernon asked Ben as they filed up the corridor out of the assembly hall together.

"Pulsar Remove. I don't suppose you have any idea where that is?" Ben replied.

"Pulsar Remove - no kidding? Mega result, man! Yes, yes yes!" Vernon danced his way along punching the air in victory as he went. "It's only *my* class, Benny boy! Listen, I'll give you the lowdown on the guys to chill out with and the ones to avoid on the way – and believe me, there are plenty of them in Pulsar Remove!"

Vernon held his 1994 Ford Fiesta up to the light and gave it a long admiring glance. Then he turned and winked at Ben. "I reckon things may begin to look up at Black Hole Primary this term."

"All right, children, settle down quickly

please. We don't have all day, you know."

"That's Miss Calculate, our maths teacher," Vernon explained as he guided Ben into the desk next to his. "She's also our form teacher."

Ben took a long, hard look at Miss Calculate. She wasn't much like any of his old teachers at Milky Way Juniors. For a start her head was shaped like a large computer monitor with a smiling face on its screen. Her hands were like calculators, with narrow rolls of print-out paper coming out where her fingers should have been.

"She's something else, huh?" Vernon obviously admired his form teacher. "She's a Zapling, you know, from the planet Zap, where everyone can do percentages and decimals and fifty-figure calculations in seconds. And what she don't know about figures ain't worth knowing, believe me. Apart from that she's harmless."

"What she *doesn't* know about figures, isn't worth knowing," Miss Calculate corrected. "You forget to tell Ben that I also have excellent hearing, Vernon. Take your seats quickly please, class, and open up your computer teletexts at page 4,057."

The whole class groaned. "What's up?" Ben asked the girl sitting on the other side of him.

"Space fractions, that's what's up!" she smirked.

"Oh yuk, time warp me to another planet," Ben moaned.

"That's Gracie - she's cool," Vernon whispered approvingly to his new friend. "She can probably do space fractions in her sleep and still come up with the right answers. And that's her best friend, Ann Droid, sitting next to her. Watch out for her systems overloads – she can burn out her main disk drive differentials if no one gets to her in time."

"Who's that funny triangular shaped boy over there?" asked Ben curiously. "I've never seen anyone quite like that before at Milky Way Juniors."

"That's Hector Vector. He's from the Planet Algebra, you know. Algebrains can change shape whenever they like, – if you ask Hector he'll show you!"

"A bit of hush please, class," Miss Calculate called out. "Orchestra wants a brief word so I hope you're all listening carefully."

"Who's Orchestra?" Ben asked Vernon.

Vernon rolled his large eyes. "Our music teacher. But don't get your cosmic underwear in an uproar. She's never heard of rap and she goes on about some dude called Beethoven all lesson long. Freaks me out, man!"

The door to the class swooshed aside with a flourish, and a robotic creature whirled in accompanied by a brief burst of the Hallelujah Chorus. She twirled a conductor's baton wildly around her head. "School concert tomorrow, everyone," Orchestra sang out. "I hope you've all been practising your instruments over the holidays, tra-la-la!"

Ben couldn't help noticing that various light bulbs lit up round her head as she spoke, and that her voice sounded like something produced by an electronic keyboard.

Ben nudged Vernon and rolled his eyes to express his amazement but stopped when he saw that Miss Calculate had spotted him.

"We'll meet up for practice later on today. Toodle-oo, my little nightingales!" Orchestra swept out of the classroom leaving a trail of tinkling notes in her wake.

"I hope you're all taking this concert seriously," Miss Calculate scolded. "In fact, for the benefit of our new boy, Ben, I will repeat the warning I gave you the end of last term. It appears that many of you are spending more time playing with your total reality computer games than you are on your studies. If this concert is an embarrassing failure for Black Hole, there is a rumour that the Head intends to confiscate all hand-held computer games immediately. Is that clear?" She stared directly at Vernon and Ben.

Everyone was silent. She means business, thought Ben. Gulp.

Ben noticed that the large, bossy Martian girl who had been pestering a smaller pupil for money during assembly had her hand in the air and was waving it about.

"Yes, Roberta Bar?" said Miss Calculate.

"I just wanted to say," the girl began forcefully, "that I'm with the Head on this one. Computer games rot the brain and when I'm form prefect tomorrow after the elections, I'm going to ban them anyway."

"That's *if* you win the election, Roberta," Miss Calculate added. "The nominations haven't closed yet, you know."

"Oh, who's going to challenge me?" the nasty girl continued. "There's no one else among this dozy collection of dishcloths to do the job, let's face it."

Roberta smiled smugly.

"Let me remind you," Miss Calculate continued, ignoring Roberta's last remark, "the class election to select a form prefect for the coming year will take place tomorrow. All nominations must be on my desk by the morning. Remember, you need one supporter to second your nomination and then votes will be cast tomorrow, after the concert."

A small electronic laser beam broke across the classroom and triggered a short, sharp siren just above the telemonitor. "Right, off you go to your first lesson of the term." Miss Calculate started to pack her things up.

Vernon sighed. "What's up?" asked Ben.

"Bad news, man, these class elections. Looks like someone already has the whole thing wrapped up."

He saw Roberta slyly pass a note to a small green Zog boy sitting just a couple of seats away. Ben peered over a couple of heads and as the Zog unwrapped the note he clearly saw the message in big clear letters: ZOG-PIG, VOTE FOR ME OR I NUKE YOUR DESK.

"Nice girl," Ben said to Vernon.

"Roberta Bar makes Attila the Hun look as soft as a wet paper bag! And she's hot favourite for the class prefect job too."

"You're not serious, are you? Who'd nominate her?" Ben looked concerned.

"Her twin brother Robbie. He's so terrified of Roberta he'll do anything she says. Hey, quit worrying, man. Loosen up, we got five minutes before Space Studies. I have some serious games practice to pack in." Vernon waved his Game-o-tronic mini-games console in front of Ben. "Only 4,000 more points to go on Fearsome Flyer, and I zoom myself into the Tronic 4-D Hologrammatic Games Hall of Fame."

Gracie packed up her books and waltzed past Vernon. "If I were you I'd get some music practice in, Vernon, or have you forgotten about the concert already?" she laughed. "I don't need a crystal ball to predict that it looks like your games-playing days are numbered!"

"No way!" cried Vernon. "The Head wouldn't dare do anything as stupid as ban computer games. He'd have one major rebellion on his hands."

Ben scratched his head thoughtfully. This Black Hole place was turning out to be the strangest school he'd come across yet.

## CHAPTER FOUR

Ben wasn't the only person feeling bewildered.

Earlier that morning his mother, a brave smile on her face and her new navy blue hat with the pink stripe on her head, had got off the number 14 interstellar bus at the Black Hole terminus, and had walked towards the warden control capsule where she had been instructed to report for her first day's duty.

The capsule had a large sign beside it warning members of the public who were unauthorised personnel to Proceed No Further, and some way beyond it was a bit of open ground pitted with small meteor craters. Beyond that spread a dingy brown fence, about two metres high. It stretched from left to right as far as the eye could see.

A small group of people, men and

women, were standing near the steps of the warden control capsule. From their uniforms it was obvious that they were Black Hole wardens either going on or coming off duty.

Ben's mum went up to them. "Excuse me," she said. "I'm Betty Gordon – I'm reporting for work. It's my first day." She felt a bit silly saying it.

"Well, you'd better go and introduce yourself to his lordship," said one of them – and Mrs Gordon was sure she heard a couple of the other wardens snigger behind her back. "He's in his den," said the warden, and he nodded towards the door of the capsule.

Betty Gordon knocked on the door. She put her head on one side, trying to hear whether anyone had said, "Come in."

She needn't have bothered: the door suddenly burst open and out came the most alarming man Mrs Gordon had ever seen in her life – including Ben's dad.

"NOW THEN NOW THEN NOW THEN!!!" screamed the man. He was enormous – well over two metres high, with a chest like a beer barrel. He had two cauliflower ears, and a nose like a boxer's that's been punched almost flat. His face was red, and there was a terrible scar running down through one of his eyebrows and on to his cheek. "AND WHAT 'AVE WE 'ERE??!!"

"Please..." stammered Mrs Gordon. "Please, I'm Mrs Gordon. Black Hole Patrol Warden number 457826 reporting for duty. Oh, I'm new here."

"Oh you are are you? – WELL GET FELL IN THEN YOU 'ORRIBLE LITTLE WOMAN!!!"

Crikey, thought Ben's mum. She looked round and could see that the other wardens had now formed themselves into a couple of lines on the dusty land behind the capsule, and she nipped off as fast as she could to join them.

The man marched down the steps of the capsule and strode over towards them. He had a small stick with a silver top to it under one arm; his warden's uniform was immaculate, and his cap had a black shiny peak and a gold band round it.

"RIGHT YOU LOT!" he suddenly bellowed. "Hallow me to introduce myself. My name is Sergeant Major Daft-Vader. *Got it??!!*"

The wardens all nodded to indicate that they had indeed got it.

"I am your commanding hofficer!!" he bellowed again. "I didn't choose to do this crummy job looking after a lot of Black

Hole wardens. I could have been something really big in the cosmic Inter-Ballistic Artillery! I could have been a Defender of the Universe, Commander Daft-Vader the Invincible, Lord of the Cosmos! But owing to some trouble with me feet I've had to be temporarily rested from military duties – so here I am. GOT IT??!!"

They all nodded again to show that they'd got it.

"GOOD! RIGHT!! We'll start with some basic training as to your duties. Your duties is to patrol this here fence," he indicated the fence behind him by pointing towards it with his silver-topped stick.

"Behind that there fence is the biggest black 'ole in the whole 'istory of creation. And it's our job to see as no one goes an' falls in it!! We do this by marching round and round it in an orderly and regimental fashion – eyes and ears alert. We're like prowling panthers ready to pounce. GOT IT??!!"

"Yes Sarge," said the warden standing next to Ben's mum.

"YES SERGEANT MAJOR DAFT-VADER, SIR!!!" roared the Sergeant Major at the poor warden, who repeated rather sheepishly, "Yes Sergeant Major Daft-Vader, Sir."

"That's better!! Now, we'll start the day with a couple of hours of marching and drill. We can't have my front line troops on patrol waddling about like something the cat's just sicked up, can we??!!"

"No Sergeant Major Daft-Vader," chorused the quaking front line troops.

"NO!! SO OFF WE GO! *LEFT RIGHT LEFT RIGHT LEFT RIGHT!!*"

"This is even worse than being at school!" said Mrs Gordon to herself as they set off.

And Ben would probably have agreed with her…

## CHAPTER FIVE

Miss Calculate switched the school corridor auto-walker from "saunter" to "quick as a flash" and she whizzed her way down towards the staffroom. First day back at school, she thought, and already there's a FUSS - Frightfully Urgent Staff Session. And she'd been looking forward to getting to grips with a tricky little nuclear physics poser that she had set herself just the other day. Outside the staffroom the tele-screen was flashing IMPORTANT STAFF SESSION IN PROGRESS. "Oh, asteroids!" she whispered crossly under her breath, "I'm late as well."

"Ah, Miss Calculate, there you are," Miss Wagstaff quipped tartly. "I was beginning to wonder if we should alert Black Hole Patrol!" She let out a loud, high giggle that quickly vanished. Something must be up, thought Miss Calculate. Even Wagstaff's a bag of nerves.

Miss Wagstaff stepped forward to signal that the meeting was about to commence. She'd changed clothes twice since assembly and was now wearing one of her own creations: a high-backed, low-necked jump-suit in supersoft alu-satin. She wheeled the Head in front of her skilfully and confidently, parking his trolley with tender loving care.

"The Head!" she announced rather grandly, and rather unnecessarily. There followed a faint wheeze and then came the Head's unmistakable crackle. "IT HAS COMET TO MY ATTENTION THAT A LARGE NUMBERING OF PUPILS ARE BRINGING THESE NEW FINGLED … ERM … "

Miss Wagstaff whispered at the trolley, "Computer games, sir."

"AH, YES," he continued, "COM-PUTER GAMES INTO MY SKULL. LET US NOT BE WASHY WISHY ABOUT THESE TECHNO TOYS. THEY ARE A MENACE TO SOCIETIP. IF TOMARROW'S CONCERTY IS A DISASTER, THEY SHALL BE BANISHED."

The Head swivelled with a quiet hiss towards Mr Stretch, the PE teacher. He had been idly longing for a cigarette while gazing in awe at Miss Wagstaff.

"AND YOU WILL BE IN CHARGE OF THE CONFRISCATIONS, MR STRETCH," hissed the Head.

Mr Stretch sprang to attention. "Yes, sir, certainly, sir."

"I SOSPECT THAT THESE AWFUEL GAMES HAVE ALREDAY TAKEN OVER. IT IS OUR DUTY TO STOP THE ROT."

Miss Wagstaff turned to Orchestra. "Oh, isn't he forceful," she sighed. "I love it

33

when he's angry."

"HAVE YOU ANYTHING FURTHER TO ODD, MISS WIGSTIFF?" the Head enquired.

"Just one thing, your majesty, I mean sir," she grovelled. "I'd like to remind everyone that the school concert is still scheduled for 4p.m. tomorrow afternoon. I'm sure Orchestra has something spectacular up her sleeve."

"Oh, dear, I hope she's not expecting *Phantom of the Opera*," said Orchestra to Dr Codger, the science teacher who was busily brushing chalk off his tweed jacket.

"I wouldn't put it past her – terrible woman," he moaned in reply.

"WHEELIE ME AWAY AND CARRY ON," boomed the Head.

Minutes later, Miss Wagstaff returned to the staffroom. There was quite a commotion.

"He's serious about this one, I'm afraid," she warned the other teachers.

"I only hope they've been practising hard at their instruments," said Zolo, the master in charge of Space Studies. "Imagine trying to confiscate all those blasted computer games."

"They'd all try and hide them, I bet," said Stretch, smoothing his hair down proudly. "It would be impossible to prise the wretched machines from their sweaty little palms."

"Maybe I could invent a gadget to track them down," suggested Zolo, looking flushed and excited. Truth was, he had quite a soft spot for Miss Wagstaff and was out to impress her.

"Well done, Zolo," Miss Wagstaff enthused. "Perhaps you could spend some more time developing your idea. I'll leave you to get on with it." She turned on her heels. "Shame you couldn't have come up with such a brillo plan, Mr Stretch," she smiled as she zapped past the PE teacher, leaving a cloud of her favourite perfume, "Nights Over Venus", hanging in the air.

Miss Wagstaff knew that both Mr Stretch and Zolo were competing for her affections. And she loved playing them off against each other.

"You creep," whispered Stretch to Zolo under his breath. "I'll get you back for this."

# CHAPTER SIX

"Hang on a micro-tick everyone, please," said Robbie loudly. "Roberta wants to say a few words."

"Arrrh, give us a break, Robbie," complained Vernon. "It *is* break time after all! I've challenged Ann Droid to a duel – best of three at Cosmic Racoon Goes Ballistic."

"Sorry, guys," said Robbie, "but I would advise you to listen…" By raising his eyebrows and pulling a face he made it obvious to the kids in Pulsar Remove that there could be big trouble from his twin sister if she wasn't obeyed.

Vernon sighed and gave in. He and Ben and the others in the class turned back from the door and returned to their desks, reluctantly.

"I dread these elections," said Gracie

under her breath to Ann. "Roberta's a
Martian pig; I know that may sound
planetist, but life at this school's bad
enough without her as form prefect. It'll
be like living in hell – only not so warm."

"Silence for your favourite candidate for
the forthcoming elections!" said Robbie
with a worried look on his face, and
Roberta rose from her desk at the front of
the class. Draped across the blackboard
was a huge banner that had the words
VOTE ROBERTA OR YOU'LL BE
SORRY scrawled across it in huge letters.

She stepped up to the front and turned to address the class.

"Crazy, man," said Vernon, "I knew she was a megahead – now she thinks she's a teacher!"

"Silence!" yelled Roberta. "I wish to speak! Pulsar Remove stands at a crossroads," she proclaimed loudly. "Either you can vote for me, and we shall all stride forward together to meet the challenges of the future that lie before us – or you can vote for some other pumped-up little air-head and it'll be a disaster; that is if any of you dares to stand against me."

"Rhubarb," whispered Gracie under her breath, "cosmic rhubarb!"

"Any questions?" said Roberta, glaring at her.

"I've got a question," said Ben. He said it rather quietly, not sure if he should or not.

"You're new here, Earthling – you don't count."

"Yo! Listen up!" yelled Vernon loudly. "Let a dude speak, will you."

"All right then, new kid, what is it?" said Roberta menacingly.

"Well," said Ben clearing his throat and feeling a bit stupid. "If we vote for you as our new form prefect, what will you do for us?"

A general murmur of approval for this question went round the room.

"Good one, man, well axed," whispered Vernon.

"LOOK, NUMBSKULL!" barked Roberta. "Ask not what I'll do for you if you vote for me – it's what I'll do *to* you if you don't! I've already got enough votes for a landslide, so I'm having this meeting just to point out what may happen to anyone is foolish enough to stand or vote against me! It's a warning, that's all!"

"Oh yeah?" said Vernon sarcastically.

"YEAH! For a start I'll ask Stretch to introduce extra gym for special new form prefect's detentions, then I'll speak to old Ma Danvers in the kitchens to serve up one of her liver and tapioca specials for kids I choose to 'reward'."

Several of the children grimaced at the very thought of this.

"There'll be wheel clamps for skateboards, road tax for bikes, fines for disobedience, solitary confinement in the chemical conveniences for as long as I choose … oh, and if I feel like it I'll introduce a special VAT – Very Aggressive Tax – on anyone who has the nerve to oppose me in the election. Now get those voting slips filled in for tomorrow – and we'll all go forward together, but with me as the leader. Meeting dismissed."

She swept out of the classroom like a rhino that's been laser zapped in a tender spot.

"Phewww …!!" said Ben in the silence that followed her departure. "Is life at this place always as bad as this?"

"Bad?" said Vernon. "Hey man – you ain't even had no lunch yet!!"

# CHAPTER SEVEN

Ben gazed down at his plate. He had never seen anything quite like this before in his life. His experience of school dinners at Milky Way Juniors had never been entirely happy. But on the other hand, he had never seriously feared for his life either.

"What do you think this is?" he asked Vernon. He was talking about the dark-grey mass that was seething silently on his plate. Every now and then small bubbles burst on its surface, leaving craters; it gave off the odour of old gym socks that have just been discovered under the bed after several weeks.

Vernon picked up something grey and extremely nasty on his fork and held it up closely to his face.

"Just a hunch," he guessed, "but I reckon it's liver stew."

"How do you work that one out?" asked Ben.

"Elementary, my dear Ben. When you've eaten Mrs Danvers' liver stew as many times as we have, you'll be able to smell it a few trillion light years away too," said Gracie.

"Who's Mrs Danvers?" Ben wondered.

"The demon of the school kitchen," explained Ann Droid. "She's still working to ancient twentieth-century recipes, I'm afraid."

"Let me tell you, they're diabolical, dude," Vernon chipped in.

"If you think this is bad, wait till you see what's for pudding," Ann laughed. The two pink antennae that stuck out from the top of her head wobbled as she giggled.

"Let me guess," said Ben "Rice pudding?"

The others laughed even louder.

"You're barking up the wrong satellite, Ben," said Vernon. "It's toffee tart."

"Toffee tart," said Ben. "Sounds OK to me."

"Last time we had that, our science master, old Dr Codger, had to have a plumber in to separate his false teeth!" sniggered Gracie.

Ben pushed his plate away from him. "Think I'll skip pudding today, thanks gang."

After lunch, Ben and Vernon made their way to a corner of the astro-playground. "What's your best ever score on Alien Alert, buddy?" Vernon asked Ben.

"Twenty-five thousand or so," said Ben. "Look, I don't mean to worry you Vernon, but aren't you nervous about tomorrow's concert? If it's a failure you stand to lose your Games-o-Tronic for at least the rest of term."

"Stay cool, Benny boy," said Vernon as he concentrated even harder on the screen in front of him, a flashing mass of colour and action. "My mum's an opera singer and my dad plays violin in an orchestra. Music is in my blood, man. Pulsar Remove will breeze through the concert – no sweat."

But Ben wasn't listening to Vernon any more. In the corner of the playground by the force field, something had caught his eye.

"What's going on over there?" he wondered.

"Over where?" said Vernon, without looking up.

"There, in the corner. Looks like Ann's

in trouble."

Vernon flipped his game on to HOLD mode and jumped up. "Let's spin into action, man."

By the time the boys arrived, Ann Droid had already keeled over.

"Can you help me get her up?" Gracie asked the boys. She was looking concerned and cradled Ann gently in her arms. "She's had another one of her systems overloads, I'm afraid."

"What brought that on?" asked Vernon. "She seemed fine to me at lunch."

"It's Roberta," sighed Gracie. "She's been trying to drum up a little support for the class election tomorrow. She told Ann that unless she voted for her, she'd chuck her random memory circuit boards into the Black Hole."

"Typical Roberta tactics," said Vernon. "Looks like we're in for a reign of terror this term."

"Could you pass me that back-up mini-generator from my rucksack, please," Gracie said to Ben.

"What are you going to do?" Ben asked as he began rummaging for the electronic gadget.

"We'll fix her, of course," Gracie said as she toyed with a plate-load of wires from Ann's internal system. "I've done it often enough in the past, haven't I, Vern?"

"It's true," agreed Vernon. "Grace is an ace with the spaghetti!"

"Seriously," said Ben. "We can't allow Roberta to carry on bullying everyone like this. If she wins that class election tomorrow, there'll be no stopping her. Why doesn't someone else stand against her?"

Ann's eyelids creaked open and she sat bolt upright.

"Like who?" she rubbed the back of her neck. "Thanks, Gracie. That feels mega-

tons better."

"Well, what about you, Gracie?"

Gracie shook her head. "Not my style, thanks, Ben. I'm happier tinkering with computers than getting stuck into class politics."

Ben turned to Vernon.

"Well, Vern, then. You'd make a brilliant candidate."

Vernon took a step backwards and held up his hands.

"No way, man – get off my case! I need my total reality computer games and my music. Don't talk to me about elections."

"Wait a minute," said Ann. "I think there may be an answer here. We're looking for

someone who's forceful without being bossy, likeable without being creepy, who doesn't belong to any particular gang and has some natural leadership qualities thrown in for good luck. Am I right?"

The others nodded.

"Well, Benny boy," she smiled, "you may be new here, but it looks like you're the guy for the job!"

## CHAPTER EIGHT

Just then, the school laser siren went off, and the children all trooped in for afternoon classes.

"What's next lesson?" Ben asked Gracie as they stood together on the school corridor auto-walker.

"Music, of course," she replied. "It's poor Orchestra's last chance to knock us into shape before tomorrow's concert!"

The music room at Black Hole Primary reminded Ben of the Very Modern Languages laboratory at his old school, Milky Way Junior. It had rows of small booths – each one with a large electronic keyboard in it.

Orchestra was already sitting in the teacher's booth when Pulsar Remove walked into the room.

She smiled, and the row of light bulbs

across the top of her head lit up and flashed. "Now then, class," she said, "this is your last chance. I'm relying on you: I hope you've all been practising like crazy – tomorrow is your big day – tarra-diddle-dee!"

She smiled again, and the room filled with the sound of hundreds of violins.

"Put on your headsets. I suggest you all play individually in turn – with your headsets tuned to Channel Eight we'll all be able to listen to each other. OK, Ann Droid – would you like to start? Select 'piano' on your keyboard, and play us *Blackbird Waltz*. Off you go."

Ben had his headset on, and tuned a large dial in front of him to Channel 8.

"Please, Miss," said Ann Droid's voice over the headset. "Please, Miss, I haven't practised *Blackbird Waltz*…"

"Why ever not, girl?!" said Orchestra crossly.

"Because last night we had to go over to see my gran, and I had too much homework Miss, and I got an overload."

"Oh, very well. Gracie - perhaps you could play *Blackbird Waltz* for us please."

A noise came out over Ben's headset that sounded a bit like a dog walking about on a piano keyboard. Not a very musical dog either. It was terrible! Some of the class started laughing.

"Enough!" shouted Orchestra. Blue sparks started to shoot from her ears, and one of the light bulbs on the top of her head popped out and shattered on the floor.

"TERRIBLE! Robbie and Roberta - play us your duet please, and be quick about it."

The noise Robbie and Roberta made was even worse than Gracie's *Blackbird Waltz*. Roberta started without waiting for her brother. She thumped the keyboard

51

mercilessly: it sounded like an elephant walking through a large drum kit. And every time Robbie played a wrong note (which was often) Roberta gave him a sneaky kick under the keyboard.

"ENOUGH!" shouted Orchestra again. She glowered in silence at the whole class as the sound of Roberta's efforts died away. Then the room began to fill with swelling funeral music – like a slow march, and Orchestra spoke: "Listen here Pulsar Remove: you are the worst prepared, laziest, most incompetent group of children I have ever had to try to teach music to. And I know what's causing it – these stupid computer games. Well, I've got news for you. We had a meeting this morning and the Head announced that if tomorrow's concert is a shambles, he will organise a mass confiscation of all computer games immediately. Maybe you'll take your practice a little more seriously from now on." She looked down at the shocked faces before her.

"Right, I suppose my last chance is Vernon - though he's such a total Nintendohead that I don't suppose he's done a moment's practice in the last month, eh Vernon?"

"Well, not really Miss: been kinda busy!" said Vernon with a wicked grin.

"Right Vernon. Play anything you like, and make it good or this class is going to be in detention that could well last into the next century – and I'm talking light years!"

The funeral march died away, and the room fell silent. From where he was sitting Ben could see Vernon in the booth in front of him.

Vernon put the mini handheld version of Super Star-Slayer back into his top pocket, and switched on his keyboard. He stood up at it and started to play.

It was magic, total magic. Ben's mouth fell open in admiration. Vernon flicked switches, and pounded away at the keyboard in a series of raps, boogies, piano riffs and cadenzas that seemed to fill the whole room with a big band rocking beat.

When he'd finished Vernon flashed a grin and sat down.

The whole class started clapping; indeed Orchestra led the applause. Her lights flashed red and yellow (a sure sign she was pleased) and the Hallelujah Chorus rose from the small speakers she wore as earrings.

"All I can say, Pulsar Remove, is thank heavens for Vernon! We'll just have to rely on him to see us through – since the rest of you are so hopeless. Thank your lucky stars for him – he's got more talent than the rest of you lot put together, tra-la-la!"

# CHAPTER NINE

When Mrs Gordon arrived home, she discovered Ben sitting in front of the mega-telescreen, flipping between forty different channels.

"What's the matter, nothing on then, dear?"

"Only the usual rubbish," sighed Ben. It all seemed to be quiz games and astro-soaps these days. His mother was a big fan of *Constellation Street*, which Ben actually quite enjoyed (not that he was about to admit it to her, though).

Mrs Gordon stood in front of the huge four metre screen and put one hand on her hip. She was pretending to be annoyed.

"Oh, hello, mother dear. Lovely to see you. How did you get on with your first day in your important new job?"

"Well, thank you for asking, Ben,

darling," she continued, swivelling the other way.

"I had a most interesting day. I found out that my new boss is a complete ogre, a tyrannical psychopath – and that my job is marching round five hundred metres of forcefield fencing that looks about as dull as a turned-off telly. I now also know that anyone who has ever drifted into the wretched black hole has never drifted out again to tell the tale."

"Really?" Ben sat up on the sofa, fascinated. "Tell me all the gory details, Mum, go on."

"Honestly, children these days," said Mrs Gordon. "It's all dematerialisation and destruction, that's all you're ever interested in. Well, as it happens, there are no gruesome details to pass on. Oh, a few people have been saved from the Black Hole – they reckon the fence itself saves about a hundred people every year – but no one has ever discovered what lies on the other side. Ooh, my feet are killing me," she complained as she slipped off her sensible patrol warden's shoes and rubbed her bunions through her tights. "Herbie's probably on the blink again – go and make me a nice cup of tea, there's a good lad."

Ben threw down the channel changer on the sofa and got up grudgingly.

Not a word about me, he thought, no asking me, "How did you get on in your first day at that awful school with a brain surgeon's nightmare repair job for a headteacher?"

As the door to the kitchen slid open automatically to allow Ben in, a wagging metallic bundle flew out, yelping wildly and trying to jump up at Ben. It was Woofer, the Gordons' auto-pet. They had only had him for two months so he was still on his puppy programme, but Mrs Gordon had been threatening to advance him on to his dog phase a little earlier. "He keeps chewing up my slippers," she moaned to their visitors.

"Get down, Woofer, and get back in the kitchen, please," Ben ordered the snapping little canine machine. "You know you're not allowed into the other room until your paws have been de-sharpened."

Woofer whimpered and turned on his heels, heading back for his basket. The best thing about auto-pets is their obedience. Plus, of course, the fact that they don't ever actually need to be fed.

Ben stood in front of the Robo-Service drinks dispenser. He pressed the button marked 'Tea' and waited a second. "Black or white, Ben?" asked the machine. "White please," replied Ben.

"Sugar, Ben?"

"No thanks. Can you serve it in the sitting room, please."

"Of course, sir."

"It's coming up, Mum," he yelled to his mother.

"Oh, thanks, love," replied Mrs Gordon, "you spoil me you know."

Just three seconds later, the tea magically materialised on Mrs Gordon's coffee table. "Ah, that's better," she said sipping gently. "Now, aren't you going to tell me about your day, Ben? Made any new friends yet?"

"Just a couple. Most of the kids in my class seem fairly normal. There's one guy called Vernon who's really cool - he plays computer games all the time and he's an ace musician too."

"Oh, put some relaxing music on the system, will you," said Mrs Gordon as she snuggled into her chair. "It's just what I need to wind down. A nice bit of Richard Clayderhosen or Monty Varnish, or maybe Bally Marrowload."

Ben crossed the room and clicked the micro-diskette into the machine. Instantly, the gooey, syrupy sound of Richard Clayderhosen tinkling the ivories filled the room. He was every mum's favourite pin-up boy with his long golden locks and his big blue eyes. Ben couldn't stand him. Richard Clayderhosen made his mother behave in a ridiculous manner.

"Oh, I wish I could play the piano like this, I really do." Mrs Gordon started running her fingers up and down an imaginary keyboard on the coffee table.

Just as well no one from school can see me now, thought Ben. They'd think my mother was completely barmy. Mrs Gordon was whirling her fingers dramatically, just about to reach an almighty crescendo. They'd probably be right, too, thought Ben. She's as loopy as a lace of liquorice.

"So what's all this you were saying about the forcefield fence?" Ben asked his mother, trying to distract her from her musical interlude.

"Oh, it's just a horrible rusty brown fence, nothing much to it really. The main problem is people who keep flying into it. They don't see it's there, apparently."

"Why don't they paint it a decent

bright colour," suggested Ben, "so that people could see it more clearly? What about a psychedelic, technicoloured fence? That would be fun!"

"Hey! Do you know, that's not such a bad idea," said Mrs Gordon surprise. "I might just have a word with big chief Daft-Vader about that tomorrow! Goodness only knows, I need to come up with something to get me in his good books. He called me 'an 'Orrible little woman' this morning!"

"Never mind, Mum," Ben said as he gave his mother a friendly hug. "It's early days yet."

"Yes," she smiled and hugged him back. "You're right. And who knows? If he likes my suggestion tomorrow, I might be his star warden on the patrol. Wouldn't that be thrilling, love?"

# CHAPTER TEN

When Ben arrived at Black Hole Primary the next morning he was still feeling shattered. What with thinking about his new friends, the concert, the weird teaching staff – and most of all the form prefect elections, he hadn't had a very good night's sleep.

Ben had lain awake thinking about Ann Droid's amazing suggestion that he should stand as a candidate against the terrible Roberta. Was it a crazy idea? After all, Ann was a humanoid robot, and humanoid robots could get systems failures and voltage fluctuations that made them come up with pretty cranky schemes... But why should the class be dominated by a tyrant like Roberta – with her Very Aggressive Tax and skateboard clamping? Ben shuddered in horror at the thought of it.

By breakfast-time Ben had been fairly certain he should take Roberta on, and by the time he met Vernon in the school entrance chamber he had made up his mind.

"Hi, Dude!" said Vernon, smiling as ever. "This could be a big day, man. I've sure got to wow them at the concert this afternoon – my life support system is on the line!" Vernon waved his Games-o-tronic at Ben.

"I want to wow them too, Vern…" said Ben.

"Whatcha goin' to play, then?" said Vernon, surprised.

"No, not at the concert. In the form election. I'm going to stand as a candidate against Roberta. It's Ann's suggestion. I'm not scared of her, and I think I'd let everyone down if I didn't have a go at it."

"Cool. Real cool!" said Vernon, taken aback.

"Will you nominate and vote for me, Vernon?"

"I'll even help you run your campaign! Great!" Vernon replied.

The two boys smacked palms and ran into the assembly hall. Unfortunately, they also ran into Roberta…

"So!" said Roberta, her hands on her hips. "Little New Boy Snivelhead is going to stand against me - accompanied by the Music Man!" She sneered at Vernon. "I think this will call for some rather creative campaigning on my part. I'm not afraid of using a few dirty tricks to stop a pair of computer-crazed kippers from ruining my chances of world domination."

The boys looked at each other as if to say, what on Jupiter is she talking about!

"Oh, yes, this isn't just a form prefect election. This is just the beginning. With a little luck and plenty of chinese burns, I reckon I can be school captain in a term or two. Then one day, I may oust that wimpy lump of jelly that calls himself the Head and take over this whole show." Roberta's eyes had glazed over and her lips turned up cruelly at the corners.

"This is my chance to shine, to make my mark. And I'm not letting a couple of soggy digestives like you two get in my way. Stand against me if you like Ben Gordon," she snarled, "but be prepared for a long, hard fight - and I'm talking dirty! That form prefectship is mine by rights and I'm not going to let some goody-two-shoes new boy just waltz in and snatch my moment of glory. Don't say I didn't warn you."

And with that, she stomped off in search of more mischief and misery-making.

# CHAPTER ELEVEN

Mr Grudge, the school caretaker, cleaner and odd-job robot, trundled slowly along the corridor to the Head's office and stopped outside. Spitting oil on his hands a few times to moisten them, he smoothed down what was left of his wispy wire hair, using the glass in the door of the Head's office as a mirror.

Slowly and deliberately, he creaked his left arm up to shoulder height and knocked sharply on the door twice.

"COME IP!" boomed the unmistakable tones of the Head from within.

Grudge pressed the entry button and the door slid quickly aside. Grudge knew it would. He had only just greased it last week in preparation for the new term. The Head always insisted that everything in his office should be in excellent working order, and Grudge was only too willing to oblige.

As Grudge stepped into the Head's office he sniffed the air, recognising the familiar perfume of Miss Wagstaff.

"Fuddlestocks," he muttered. "What's that interfering Deputy Head doing here?" Ideas above her airport, that's her trouble, thought Grudge.

"Do take a pew, Mr Grudge." Miss Wagstaff pointed towards one of the uncomfortable chairs and settled herself down into one of the Head's luxuriously padded superseaters. They're for the benefit of the school governors, not some jumped up little knitting pattern like you, thought Grudge to himself.

"The Head would like a quick word in your earback," explained Miss Wagstaff.

"What's that you say?" said Grudge, putting his hand to his ear. He always pretended to be deaf when Miss Wagstaff spoke to him. He knew it annoyed her because he never asked the Head to repeat anything. Of course, with a voice like the Head's, no one ever needed to ask him to repeat anything. Even schools a strato-sphere away were said to have picked up the Head's speech waves during a couple of his especially fearsome assemblies.

"The Head would like a word with you, Mr Grudge," screeched Miss Wagstaff at full throttle. Even the Head looked alarmed at the dramatic increase in volume.

"All right, all right, no need to shout. I'm not flapping deaf, you know," moaned Grudge.

"Then may I suggest that you have your hearing and perception systems overhauled at the next possible opportunity," snarled Miss Wagstaff. "I seem to have to repeat everything for you these days."

Grudge chuckled to himself inside. Really getting on her wick today, aren't you, Grudgey, he thought.

"I HAVE A LITTLE FAVIP TO ASK OF YOU, GRUDGE," boomed the Head.

Mr Grudge almost hit the roof. The Head's terrifying voice always came as something of a shock to him, even when he expected it.

"And what might that be then, Sir? I've served you – and the school of course – in my present capacity for many a millennium now, and in all those years, I don't think I've ever said no to one of your little favours in the past." Excellent creeping, Grudgey-boy, he thought to himself. I'll show that Wagstaff that when it comes to crawling, she's a complete amateur.

"I'VE HAD SARGEN MAJICK DAFT-VADER ON THE TELESCREEN THIS MORNING. ONE OF HIS NEW WARDENS HAS SERGESTIPT THAT IT WOULD BE A GOOG IDEA TO RE-PAINT THE FORCEFIELD FENCE, BRIGHTIP UP A BIT."

Grudge's greasy grey metallic face dropped a couple of kilometres. Not that blooming fence, he thought, not *that* old chestnut.

"And the Head and I agree that this is a splendid idea," smirked Miss Wagstaff. "I can see it now," she continued, rising from her chair and stretching her hand out before her in a creative gesture. Cripes, here we go, thought Grudge. She's off again.

"We'll use it as an opportunity to show the galaxy just how artistic we are at Black Hole Primary. The new fence will be a riot of psychedelic colours inspired by some of the more unconventional hues in this firmament we call our home…"

"What's that mean in plain English?" chipped in Grudge.

"Vivid orange, neon green, fluorescent yellow, dayglo magenta…" Miss Wagstaff was waxing lyrical.

"…pukey pine?" suggested Grudge unhelpfully.

"Thank you, Mr Grudge," said Miss Wagstaff, giving him one of her famous withering looks, "but I'm sure I can work out the colour scheme for myself."

"Suit yourself," Grudge grumbled into his dirty old moustache.

"YOU WILL STARP AS SOON AS PUSSOBLE," said the Head. "MUCH APPRECIATE THIS, GRUDGE. DON'T FORGUT TO CLOSE THE DIRE ON YOUR WAY OUT."

Grudge looked up in amazement. Why, the crafty old devil, he thought. He's not even going to give me the chance to say no.

Miss Wagstaff waved a hand dismissively at the caretaker.

"You may go, Mr Grudge," she smirked. "I'm sure you'd like to get started immediately."

"Oh, I can hardly contain my joy," whinged Grudge as he rose slowly with a series of squeaks. "I shouldn't be doing this sort of thing, not at my age," he continued. "I could do myself a nasty damage painting kilometres of dirty old fencing. Me joints is racked with rust and arthritis as it is."

"Black Hole Patrol..." he muttered, as he stomped back down the corridor, "bunch of time-wasters more like."

## CHAPTER TWELVE

Back in Pulsar Remove, Miss Calculate was just taking the auto-register.

"Right," she declared when the last barcode had been read in, "now it's time to close the nominations for form prefect. So far," she continued, holding a piece of paper aloft with the word, 'Roberta' scrawled on it in thick black foil-tip pen, "I only have one nomination, and that is Roberta's. Are there any more candidates?"

Ben shifted uneasily in his seat.

"You sure you know what you're doing, man?" Vernon inquired anxiously. "Unleash the wrath of Roberta and you could be in deep, deep trouble."

"No, it's not fair," Ben said decisively. "She's just a bully and someone has to stand up to her. Nominate me, Vern."

Vernon pushed his shiny desk away from

him and stood up. He was one of the tallest in the class and all eyes were locked in his direction.

"I have a nomination," said Vernon in a cool, clear voice. "I nominate Ben Gordon."

Roberta jumped up in a trice.

"Ben Gordon! Ben Gordon!" she screeched. "He hasn't even been in this school five minutes and already he thinks he can run the place."

"Roberta, please! Sit down this millisecond!" Miss Calculate called out. "May I remind you that the rules concerning form prefect as laid down by the Head are quite clear. Candidates must be members of the class and they need to be nominated by one pupil and seconded by another. Ben may be a new addition to our class, but I see no reason why he shouldn't stand if he wishes. Now Vernon has nominated Ben. Will anyone second him?"

There was a moment's silence. Suddenly a nervous little voice rang out from the back of the class.

"Yes, I will."

It was Ann Droid. She was visibly shaking, trying not to look in Roberta's direction.

"Very well," declared Miss Calculate. "If there are no other nominees, I hereby declare that Roberta Bar and Ben Gordon are officially nominated as candidates for the form prefectship of Pulsar Remove. Elections will take place at end of school this afternoon. Now, where were we? Multiplication in the fifth dimension, wasn't it?"

Ann looked down at the mathematics module on the screen in front of her. She felt sure that Roberta was staring directly at her, but she dare not look up just yet. After five minutes or so, she threw a quick glance in Roberta's direction and, sure enough, the beastly bully was glowering straight at Ann.

She mouthed the words, "I'll get you later," and then looked away. Ben caught sight of Ann.

"Thanks for seconding me," he smiled. "Don't worry. If Roberta wants to pick a fight she can start with me."

As the laser siren rang out for the end of their lesson, Roberta collared her twin brother Robbie and dragged him to one side.

"I want to talk to you about my campaign, Mr Wimpo, and that means right now. Understand?"

Robbie Bar squirmed madly, trying to escape from his sister's grasp.

Finally, he gave up.

"All right, all right, what do you want?"

"Not here, dummy! Somewhere where supersonic ears won't hear us. Over by the perimeter fence - MOVE IT!"

"Right," Roberta said through clenched teeth as she stood with her back to the dirty old fence. "Have you distributed my pamphlets? Have you put up my lovely VOTE ROBERTA OR I NUKE YOUR DESK posters? Have you carried out any extremely painful tortures as I suggested?"

Robbie shook his head. To tell the truth, he was just as scared of his sister as everyone else. He didn't want her to win the class election any more than anyone else in Pulsar Remove. She was bossy enough as it was.

"This election isn't going to be won without a little effort from you, you lazy limp lettuce leaf!" raged Roberta. "Get going right now. Drum up support. Give the weedy ones some painful pinches, threaten the wimps with tarantulas, set fire to a few exercise books. That should do the trick. Remember, if I don't win this election today, I shall be holding you personally responsible. Now get out of my sight."

Robbie scarpered pretty sharpish, leaving Roberta pondering by the fence. Why that blasted Ben Gordon? she thought. Yesterday morning, I had this whole election sewn up. Now that interfering do-gooder has put the mockers on everything. Roberta was getting madder and madder, her heavy Martian features wrinkling up with anger as she worked herself into a top-grade lather. Looking up, she noticed Grudge just a few metres away painting the fence. Balancing on top of the rusty forcefield were some mucky old pots filled with different coloured paints. Roberta shouted out, "Have you got your false teeth in today, rust bucket?"

Grudge looked up from his handiwork, turning towards the school to see who was shouting abuse at him. "'Orrible little crisps," he muttered under his breath. "They'd all be sold for science experiments if I had my way."

Roberta gave the fence a good kick. She was mad and she wanted someone else to suffer even if it was only that mechanical mishap of a school caretaker. She gave the fence a second even harder kick. This one's for you, Ben Gordon, she thought. And lo and behold, the second kick did the trick. Several of the pots that were balancing on top of the fence slipped over the edge and glided down the gaping void of the Black Hole . . .

# CHAPTER THIRTEEN

Orchestra raced down the school corridor at the speed of light. Quick, she thought, must get Miss Wagstaff. No time to waste.

She launched herself into Miss Wagstaff's office without even knocking at the door.

"Oh, Miss Wagstaff, thank goodness you're here. Do come quickly! There's the most awful commotion coming from the school kitchen. I fear there may be some sort of nuclear reaction taking place in there."

"Nuclear reaction?" Miss Wagstaff stood up to her full height. She had just been laser-sketching some ideas for a new trousersuit in a super-light, heat resistant foil-effect fabric and was planning how she would wear her hair with the snazzy new outfit. She wasn't best pleased at being interrupted by the sight of the school music

78

teacher in a right old tizz.

"Calm down, Orchestra, please. I think the idea of this afternoon's school concert has made you a little edgy. Now tell me slowly and clearly, what on Jupiter is going on here?"

"It's the kitchen," explained Orchestra desperately. "I don't know what's going on in there but it's louder than Beethoven's Fifth. Oh come quickly, do, Miss Wagstaff. I think the whole school could be in mortal danger. Perhaps we are all being sucked into the Black Hole."

"Oh, what a ridiculous notion," said Miss Wagstaff. "Still, I suppose I'd better take a look." Miss Wagstaff sighed and pushed her designs to one side. What a pity my art always has to suffer in the face of a crisis, she thought.

Miss Wagstaff stood outside the kitchen and took a deep breath. From behind the door came the terrible sound of massive crash after massive crash, followed by a series of screams and wails. "Either someone is being murdered in there, or there has been a serious explosion." She turned to Orchestra. "I'm going in."

"Oh but you can't risk your own life for the sake of the school," cried Orchestra.

"Think - you may be sacrificing a brilliant career, a passion for ponchos, free luncheon vouchers every week."

Miss Wagstaff had a look of grim determination on her face. You're the youngest deputy head in the western galaxy, she told herself. And now is your chance to prove what a gutsy teacher you are.

"Stand aside, Orchestra," she ordered the music teacher, and then added rather dramatically, "a teacher's got to do what a teacher's got to do."

At the flick of a switch the door to the kitchen flew aside. Miss Wagstaff was greeted by an amazing sight. There, in the middle of the kitchen floor, sat the school cook, Mrs Danvers, covered from head to toe in flour and treacle. Her massive frame was shaking with rage and she was screeching like an atomic alleycat.

"Why, whatever is going on here?" Miss Wagstaff quaked. (To tell the truth, she was always a little wary of Mrs Danvers – even at the best of times. But she'd never seen her like this before.) "Are you injured, Mrs Danvers?" For a moment, Miss Wagstaff thought Mrs Danvers was in serious danger of exploding.

"Someone," she screeched, her whole body shuddering with fury and her huge mouth opening almost as wide as the Black Hole, "SOMEONE HAS PINCHED ME VERY BEST PANS!"

"Pans?" said Miss Wagstaff with a look of disbelief, not quite able to catch the meaning of the word. "Pans? You mean the things people use for cooking?"

"Of course, I do, you nithead!" spluttered Mrs Danvers. "What other type of pans is there?"

Miss Wagstaff was appalled, but managed to resist the temptation to reprimand Mrs Danvers for being so cheeky. "And did these criminals wreak this havoc and coat you in ingredients as well?" She pointed at the gunge that covered the school cook.

"Oh, don't be ridiculous!" shouted Mrs Danvers, "I made a little mess trying to find my pans, that's all."

Pans. That word again. It set Mrs Danvers off once more, gasping for air as she wailed.

"They've gone, I tell you. It's the crime of the century. The shiniest, sheeniest, most beautiful set of saucepans you ever did see, made of the finest zircate from the planet Pluto. Non-stick, non-rust, non-corrosive, and now they're non-existent. Some snivelling space thief has snitched the the lot.

"Oh, wait till I get my hands on the culprits, I'll teach them to mess with Gladys Danvers. I'll, I'll..." Mrs Danvers' mind was racing in a desperate search to come up with a suitable punishment for the dreadful deed. Suddenly, a twinkle came to her eye and she looked up triumphantly.

"I'll make bolognese of them, that's what I'll do!"

Urgh, thought Miss Wagstaff, there's an unappetising thought. She's put me right off pasta for the rest of the term.

"Come, come, now, Mrs Danvers," Miss Wagstaff tried to reassure the crazed chef, "I'm sure we can find you some other pans."

Underneath all the flour, Mrs Danvers was red with rage.

"Are you completely stupid?" she boomed. "I've already told you, I don't want any old pans. I want my best set back." And with that she let out a long, low sob, and collapsed in a heap scattering treacle and tears all over the floor.

What did they teach us on the school management teaching course? thought Miss Wagstaff as she racked her brains desperately. Yes, be positive, that was it.

Never give in.

"I'll organise a search party immediately," Miss Wagstaff said in what she hoped was a very cheerful voice. "I'm sure we'll have your pans back in no time at all, Mrs Danvers."

"B-b-b-but I want them b-b-b-b-back NOW," she wailed uncontrollably, then added with a vicious flourish, "and what's more, I'm on strike. The kitchen remains shut until they're returned."

Well, every cloud has a silver lining, thought Miss Wagstaff. That's possibly the best news I've had all morning.

"Orchestra," Miss Wagstaff called to the music teacher who still stood trembling outside the door. "Could you please come in here and help get Mrs Danvers cleaned up? She's suffered a dreadful loss this morning. Her pans," she mouthed to Orchestra who nodded understandingly.

"In the meantime," said Miss Wagstaff, "I'd better try and find some food for the school."

"Does that mean Mrs Danvers won't be cooking today?" Orchestra asked hopefully.

"I'm afraid not," said Miss Wagstaff, trying her best to look upset at the thought.

"It looks like I'm going to have to make other arrangements."

"And what exactly do you have in mind?" demanded Mrs Danvers, wiping a floury tear from her eye and screwing her face up in a threatening manner.

"I'm sending for Captain Codling's Cosmic Fish and Chip Rocket," said Miss Wagstaff firmly.

# CHAPTER FOURTEEN

It was the last lesson before lunch, and Pulsar Remove were getting to grips with Space Domestic Science with Zolo. This morning they were learning how to make Moon Rock Cakes when suddenly the children of Black Hole Primary heard an unfamiliar though welcome sound.

"DEE DUM DEE DUM DIDDY DUM DEE DUM, DIDDY DUM, DEE DUM, DIDDY DUM DEE DUM."

"Hey," said Hector, looking up from his cake mixture, "that's *Greensleeves*. Captain Codling's Cosmic Fish and Chip Rocket!"

"He's right!" said Gracie.

"What's going on?" said several others in the class.

"Oh, yes, I forgot to tell you," said Zolo. "I'm afraid we have some rather bad news." A smile lit up his deep-purple face. "Mrs

Danvers in the school kitchen went on strike this morning – something about having her equipment nicked, I gather."

"Does that mean she won't cook lunch?" said Gracie, looking eager.

"Yes, I'm afraid it does," replied Zolo, trying his best not to smile.

"Hurrah! Yaay! Brillo!!" yelled the kids.

"I knew you'd be disappointed" said Zolo, the merest hint of a smile creeping into the corners of his mouth. "The wonderful Miss Wagstaff has sent for the fish and chip rocket."

The children were cheering so loudly at this good news that they only just managed to hear the morning's final laser alarm, summoning them to the dining hall for lunch.

Through the school window they could see Captain Codling and his famous chippie rocket parked of the edge of the astro-turf playing field. They could see Miss Wagstaff, and Mrs McTavish, the school secretary, leaning in through the window in the side of the rocket.

"Space plaice and chips three hundred and fifty seven times please Captain Codling," said Miss Wagstaff.

"Chips silicon or potato?"

"Oh, potato please."

"Salt and vinegar?"

"Yes, please."

"Space plaice and potato chips three hundred and fifty seven times coming up!" said Captain Codling, "with salt and vinegar."

And so it was that, not many minutes later, three hundred and fifty-something smiling children and teachers were sitting down in the Black Hole Primary dining hall, unwrapping the best school lunch any of them could remember.

As Ben tucked into his chips, he turned to Gracie.

"Gracie, do you know where Vernon is? I haven't seen him around since Space Domestic Science."

"Knowing Vernon he's probably off in some corner of the school fiddling with his Games-o-Tronic hand set," she said licking the salt and vinegar from her fingers. "Mm, best school lunch I've ever had!"

"I'm not so sure," said Ben.

"Well you don't know him as well as we do," added Ann, and for a moment or two they ate their chips in silence.

It's OK for them, thought Ben to himself. I need Vernon to help fight my campaign against Roberta. Without his support I probably won't get any votes at all! Horror struck him as he realised what Roberta would do to him, in particular, when she swept to victory.

Just then, another horrible thought struck Ben as well.

"Do you realise that without Vernon we're totally sunk for the concert this afternoon?" Ben reminded Ann and Gracie.

"I'm sure he'll turn up soon," said Ann. "After all, if he doesn't it means no more total reality computer games for a very long time. I can't imagine Vern relishing that prospect!"

"Yes, I suppose you're right," said Ben. "I'm just worried about him, that's all. Vern's already become a really good friend to me."

The three of them exchanged worried looks. "You don't think he might have gone too near the...the Black Hole," said Ann suddenly.

"Surely the wardens are there to stop things that like that?" said Ben. He was trying to imagine his mum pulling Vernon back bravely from the powerful suction of the Hole's deadly vacuum, but it was stretching his imagination to its limits. Silently, the group set about finishing their fish and chips while each of them secretly worried about their absent friend.

Round the corner of the kitchens, Robbie appeared furtively. He was clutching a pile of papers in his right hand and he suddenly started waving them frantically above his head. In his left hand was a small box.

"Read all about it! Roberta's campaign pledges. Vote Roberta and you're on to a winner!"

"I don't know why you're always so keen to help that troublesome twin sister of yours, Robbie," said Gracie as she took a leaflet from Robbie's hand. "I can't think what she's ever given you in the past."

"Oh, I don't know," said Ann. "She's given him the odd black eye!"

"It's about time you stood up for yourself," Gracie continued. "Why don't you tell her to run her own election campaign? I bet she wasn't up all night printing these leaflets."

Gracie was right, as usual. You only had to take one look at the huge bags under Robbie's eyes to know that while Roberta was getting her all-important beauty sleep last night, her twin was designing, printing and running off a whole batch of campaign leaflets.

"I have a tarantula in this box," Robbie squealed in desperation. "If you don't all vote for Roberta, I'll set it on you!"

Gracie giggled. "You're more scared of spiders than anyone! How did you get it in the box, Robbie? Tempt it with a Cosmic Pasty?!"

Hector snatched the box from Robbie's grasp and as the two boys struggled, it fell open.

Out dropped the weediest looking spider anyone had ever seen: a few pipecleaners twisted together with a couple of drawing pins for eyes.

The crowd of children began to laugh.

"You don't make a very good henchman, you know, Robbie," laughed Ben.

"Why do you let Roberta push you around like that? You do have a mind of your own, you know. You must realise that if Roberta wins she's going to be bossing you about even more than usual. It'll be 'do this, Robbie, do that, Robbie' every minute of the day. In fact," he added, winking at Gracie and Ann, "that's another very good reason why you should vote for me and NOT Roberta!"

Robbie held up his hands full of pamphlets in a hopeless gesture of despair. "She'd kill me if she thought I was even thinking about voting for you, Ben. She's already threatened to set fire to my skateboard if I don't get rid of all these pamphlets by the end of lunch."

"Here, I'll give you a hand," said Ben and, taking a handful of leaflets from Robbie, he put them on top of the remains of his fish and chips and scrunched them up with the old chip paper, so that they were concealed inside the greasy parcel. Gracie and Ann followed suit, laughing.

"Getting up to all sorts of dirty tricks, are we, New Boy Ben," said Roberta. None of them had seen her appear beside her twin – just in time to watch her leaflets turned into kitchen waste. Not that she seemed unduly worried. In fact, she was wearing a rather self-satisfied smirk on her face, almost the size of the Black Hole that lay just beyond the safety of the school fence.

"Well, it may interest you to know that everyone I have spoken to in Pulsar Remove has already agreed to vote for me," Roberta continued. "I don't know why you don't just drop out now and spare yourself the humiliation of a crushing defeat."

"Not everyone, Roberta," said Gracie speaking out bravely. "I'm voting for Ben."

"And me too," said Ann, flashing her voice connector.

"YOU!" Roberta spun around in a fury to face the young android, "YOU promised to vote for me yesterday, you little turncoat. And then you have the nerve to stand up this morning and second this" – she pointed at Ben – "this moron. Maybe androids don't have to keep their promises like Martians."

"You hurt me," said Ann, tears welling up in her large egg-shaped eyes. "I didn't have any choice."

"Leave her alone," said Ben, speaking up. He was worried that Ann might be heading for another one of her systems overloads. "You've done enough bullying for one day, Roberta."

"Well, vote for your new boyfriend then, girlies," Roberta said mimicking a sugary sweet voice, and then added with a snort, "but I won't forget this. And here's another little campaign pledge for you to think about. I'm already planning a few regular class chores for any dipsticks stupid enough not to vote for me. And I've plenty of nasty little jobs lined up for a bunch of bozos like you." Roberta grabbed Robbie by the collar of his blazer and steered him away.

"Oh, talking of your cronies, I haven't seen that little twerp Vernon around this afternoon," Roberta shouted over her shoulder. "Looks like you've lost another vote there, Benny boy."

"If I weren't so worried about this afternoon's concert, I think I might be upset by Roberta's threats," said Ann. The whole gang had organised a search party of the school grounds and there was definitely no sign of Vernon. Hector Vector had scrunched himself up into a tiny ball to check all the corners of the school, but there was no trace of Pulsar Remove's one and only musical talent.

"I don't suppose you can play the piano, Ben?" asked Gracie hopefully.

"I'm afraid I can hardly even play the music system," said Ben. But then an idea struck him. It was a big, brave, bold idea and it caused his eyes to widen somewhat, and his jaw to drop open. "Wait a minute ... I think I've just thought of something that might save everyone's games consoles from the Head's greedy grasp ... but I'll need some help."

Minutes later Ben was jumping on his solar scooter and sneaking out of the back gates, heading for home. "Back in a few minutes," he assured Gracie and Ann. "Meanwhile, you'd better get everything ready for this afternoon."

Gracie started rifling through her schoolbag. "Now what did I do with that screwdriver?" she sighed. "Ah, there it is. Look, relax, Ann, this isn't going to hurt a bit. I'll have your back off in no time at all."

"I'm not sure about this plan of Ben's, Gracie," Ann wailed, "what if it all goes wrong? I could end up blown into the next constellation."

"Nonsense," Gracie said with a mouthful of screws, "I know what I'm doing. Now, I'm just disconnecting your power supply. You won't feel a thing, honest."

With that, the continuous humming

noise that signalled activity in her android friend gradually faded. And then all was quiet.

Gracie checked her crystal watch. It could tell the time in fifty-eight different zones scattered across the galaxy, but at the moment she was only bothered about how long she had before they were due back in class.

"Ten minutes," she said to herself. "It's going to be tight, but I reckon I can do it. Come on Ben, hurry back. We haven't got a milli-second to waste!"

# CHAPTER FIFTEEN

The children of Black Hole Primary, waiting in the darkness behind the curtains of the school hall stage, were nervous. They spoke in hushed whispers.

"Can you see my mum?" one said to Gracie, who was peeping behind the back of the curtain at the audience.

"Yeah," said Gracie – "she's wearing a hat decorated with cherries."

"Bad luck ... " said the first child's friend.

"All in all I reckon it's a good thing my mum's still on Black Hole Patrol, and isn't here," said Ben to Ann Droid. At Milky Way Juniors Ben had always rather liked it when his mother had come up to the school to see him sing or be in a play. She'd sit near the front and smile stupidly at him. But today there was too much at stake and anyway she might well rumble what Ben, Gracie and Ann were up to!

"Don't worry, Ben – it can't go wrong," said Gracie. "I've double checked everything – it's all technologically sound, even though I say it myself."

On the other side of the curtain the hall was slowly filling up. Roberta and Robbie's parents came in and sat with other Martians quite near the front (Martians are inclined to be rather pushy). Gracie spotted her dad. She wanted to wave through the curtains to him, but knew that he'd never spot her small pink hand.

"Hey!" she whispered urgently. "Look, there's Vernon's mum and dad – and his sister."

"That means he can't have gone home," said Ann. "They'd have seen him and brought him back. Vernon's mum's quite fierce!"

"Strange…" said Gracie, puzzled. "They must think he's here…"

Finally the hall was full. Grudge the caretaker was at the back of the hall, and he pressed the buttons that closed the doors and drew curtains across them too.

The audience was hushed, and lights went dim and the stage curtains juddered apart.

"Make way children, please!" said Miss Wagstaff, and she brushed past them with the Head on his trolley. She was dressed from head to toe in reflective purple foil with dayglo lime-green accessories.

But she didn't look as bad as the Head did. Ben hadn't had the misfortune to be this close to the ghastly trolley before, and it almost made him sick. There on the top of it, under the glass dome, was the brain that ran Black Hole Primary. It was the colour of porridge, and looked jellyfishy slimy – its pale yellow eye swivelling this way and that.

Miss Wagstaff pushed the trolley to the centre of the stage and spoke: "Good afternoon to all of you. The Head would like to say a few words."

"GOOG AFTERNOOP," said the

crackling trolley. "AND WELCOMET TO ALL PARENTS AND FRENNS OF BLAG HOLE PRIMARIP. WE HOPE YOU ENJOYN OUR ANNUAL CONCERP. I KNOW THE PUPIPS HAVE BEEN PRACTISING HARDLY FOR IT."

Ben looked at Gracie and Gracie looked at Ben. They both looked at Ann, and all three of them looked worried.

"TO START US OFF A WARM WELCOMET PLEASE FOR OUR REMARKABUBBLE MUSIC TEACHIP, ORCHESTRA!"

Grudge flicked a light switch, a beam of white light fell in a large circle on the curtain at the side of the stage, and Orchestra stepped out from behind the curtains. The audience clapped and she smiled at them and the lights on her head lit up in orange and yellow: "Good afternoon everyone. We're going to start our little concert for you with some singing from the infant classes. Then Zog from the third year will recite a poem, and before the interval we've a wonderful piano solo for you from Pulsar Remove.

After a quick break, the infants will perform a short play, and then the Ballet Club will dance to a selection of tunes from *Saturn Lake* and *Romeo and Jupiter*. All costumes are, of course, designed by our very own Miss Wagstaff. Thank you..."

The stage lights came on and Orchestra, now behind the curtain again, hissed: "Infants - on stage please!"

The infants sang some terrible songs, and Zog from the third year recited a long poem. While he was doing this Ben had an urgent conversation with Orchestra in the darkness of the stage wings.

"Please Miss..." he began.

"Fiddle-dee-dee. What is it, dear?" said Orchestra.

"Please...Vernon's not here!"

"WHAT??!!!" Some of her lightbulbs started flashing rather dramatically and one went pop.

"He's not here. We don't know where he is – but please, I'm new at this school, but I can play the piano just as well as Vernon. I'll do the solo."

"Well..." Orchestra didn't know what to do. "Well, all right. We don't seem to have much choice, do we? I certainly can't let anyone else from Pulsar Remove near the instruments. I suppose you'll have to."

"Ann Droid says she'll help me – she'll turn the pages of my music for me."

"Yes, yes, OK," said Orchestra, still flustered.

Moments later, when Zog of the third year had finished his poem and had received polite applause, Ben was sitting on his own in the middle of the Black Hole Primary stage at the piano. A spotlight beamed down him from above and Ann Droid the humanoid robot was standing beside him with a large book of music – not a note of which Ben could understand.

There was more polite applause from the audience, and as it died away Ben whispered to Ann, "Are you ready?"

"Yes, ready," she whispered back.

Ann put the music up in front of Ben on the piano and opened it.

Ben put his hands on the keys, but not until he'd pressed a new button on the sensor pad on the back of Ann's right hand.

The moment he did, something remarkable happened.

# CHAPTER SIXTEEN

Ben's fingers rippled up and down the keyboard and the hall filled with the most wonderful music!

The parents couldn't believe their ears, and neither could Black Hole's pupils. Nor could Orchestra. She hadn't heard playing like that in any school before. Why, it was as good as a professional grown-up pianist – a professional grown-up pianist like, for instance … Richard Clayderhosen.

Even the Head, on his trolley on the edge of the stage, seemed impressed. His eye swivelled round extra fast.

Ann Droid, standing beside Ben, leaned forward and turned a page of music now and again, but she didn't seem to be concentrating very hard. She had her eyes closed most of the time, and a dreamy, faraway look had come over her face.

When Ben finished there was a deafening round of applause from the audience. He had to stand up and bow several times – the audience stood up to cheer and applaud even harder.

Finally, however, the stage curtains closed. Ben reached forward and touched the button on the back of Ann's hand, and left the stage. The first person he met in the wings was Vernon.

"Nice playing, Benny boy," chuckled his long-lost friend. "I never knew you had so much talent."

"Vernon! Where on Pluto have you been? We've been looking everywhere for you."

Vernon turned around to show Ben his hands. They were tied together behind his back.

"Someone didn't want me to play at the concert," he explained. "On my way to lunch I was grabbed from behind by someone who tied up my hands and bundled me into one of Mr Stretch's sports lockers. I only just managed to get out!"

"But you've been missing for hours," said Ben.

"You try getting a door open using just your feet, man. It ain't no picnic, believe me, dude!" said Vernon. "By the way, how did you learn to play like that? You made me look like a complete amateur."

"Easy peasy," explained Ben. "Gracie wired Ann Droid up to a couple of speakers and rigged up a diskette drive in her random memory banks. All I had to do was pretend to play while she turned on my mum's favourite hits by Richard Clayderhosen which I nipped home to fetch. It went down a bomb with the audience," added Ben, as if he did this sort of thing at school every day.

"Cool result, guys," said Vernon, slapping hands with them. "Mega cool result!"

"Listen, boys, I hate to break up the reunion but we can't hang about here," reminded Gracie. "We've got to get Ann's back panel off and sort her out quick."

As Gracie led Ann away, the familiar sound of the Head's squeaky trolley signalled his arrival.

"This is the boy," Miss Wagstaff was saying, as she pointed out Ben, surrounded by admiring children from Pulsar Remove and other classes.

"I understand he's called Ben Gordon." The children moved aside, and next thing Ben knew, he was face to face with that big wobbly jelly himself – the Head.

"WOLL DONE, BIN. TIP CLOSS PIANIP PLOYING. DO TILL ME, WHAT IS THE SOCRET OF YOURSICKCESS?"

Ben took a deep breath. Yikes, he thought, I'll have to talk my way out of this one. Suddenly, a brilliant idea struck him.

"Computer games, sir," Ben announced proudly. "I find they help sharpen my reactions and make my fingers more supple.

They've helped my keyboard skills no end."

Ben flexed his fingers a couple of times to illustrate the point.

"ROLLY?" roared the Head. "AND I WAS GOVEN TO OVERSTAND THAT THESE COMPUTY GAMES WERE ALL A LOAD OF CODSPLOPPERS. HOW INTERESTING. WHEEL ME AWOY, WIGSTIFF!" And with that, the odd couple squeaked off into the distance.

# CHAPTER SEVENTEEN

As the gang hurried back to their classroom, they began to unravel the mystery of Vernon's disappearance.

"Who do you think it was, Vern? Who would have wanted to lock you up in the sports cupboard?" asked Ben.

"It must have been whoever was standing behind me as we went to lunch. Can anyone remember who that was?"

Ann started to look a little anxious. "Actually, Vern, I think I can remember who was behind you on the way to lunch. I'm sure it was Roberta. You see, she had been giving me such dirty looks I kept turning around to check out where she was just in case she had any little tricks up her sleeve."

"Well, it certainly looks like she had one nasty little plan on her mind," said Hector.

"Sabotage the concert and get our computer games confiscated."

"And take care of my campaign manager in one fell swoop," added Ben.

"Talk about dirty tricks. Roberta must have written the book."

The children stepped off the auto-walker right outside their class. Gracie pressed the button and the door swept aside.

"Well, here's our chance to get even the fair way," she announced. "Class elections here we come – and I know who I'm voting for!"

Roberta was standing on the platform at the front of the class as the children entered.

"Hurry up and sit down, will you," she scolded as they arrived. "Let's get this thing over and done with. Once I win this election I'll have a million and one things to get sorted."

"She gets more like a teacher every day," Ann whispered to Gracie.

"Frightening, isn't it?"

As Vernon walked in, the smile soon vanished from Roberta's face.

"You!" she screamed. "What are you doing here?" Suddenly, Roberta realised

111

she was giving away her guilty secret.

"What do you mean, Roberta? Where did you imagine Vernon was?" asked Gracie with a wicked glint in her eyes.

"W-W-What I mean is, I-I-I thought you'd gone home."

Vernon gave Roberta a satisfied "foiled your little plan, haven't I?" kind of look.

"Oh, I just got a little tied up, Roberta," explained Vernon coolly. "I'm sure you know how it is."

"Now before you finally decide who your prefect is going to be, I'd like to invite Roberta and Ben up to the front to give one final speech to the class," said Miss Calculate.

Roberta stood up immediately. Ben turned to Vernon.

"What with the concert this afternoon, I'd completely forgotten about this," said Ben in a panic. "Vern - help! What am I going to say?"

Vernon put his hand on his friend's shoulder.

"Listen, Ben, my main man. You're going to make the best form prefect Black Hole has ever seen. Don't go making silly promises like Roberta. Just be yourself and tell it like it is. You'll do just fine."

Roberta had opened a huge wad of notes at the front of the class.

"You only have two minutes," Miss Calculate reminded the stroppy young Martian. "There won't be time for a lecture, Roberta."

Roberta scowled.

"Oh, all right then. Well listen to this, Pulsar Remove. I've been at this school for ages and that blithering buffoon Ben Gordon has only been around Black Hole country for five minutes. He knows nothing about this place and I bet he doesn't even know half your names. What I'm saying is this. If you vote for him, you don't know what you're going to get. Vote for me and you know what you're getting..."

Gracie turned to Ann. "A complete monster of a form prefect, that's what!"

"... you're getting honesty, reliability and trust." Roberta picked her nose absent-mindedly and ruffled her notes.

"Oh, and by the way, anyone who doesn't vote for me – and believe me, I'll find out your names – anyone who doesn't vote for me will spend the rest of the term doing toilet duty and supervising the infants' annual Christmas concert, and we all know what a torture that is, don't we?" And with that she stomped back to her desk.

Now it was Ben's turn. He stood up nervously and looked around the class.

"Maybe I have only been here for two days," Ben began, "but in those two days, I've made some of the best friends a guy could ever wish for. Gracie, Hector, Ann ... " The embarrassed android blushed to the roots of her metallic hairdo as Ben mentioned her name. "Robbie, Sarita, Henry ... " Ben looked round at each member of the class and called out his or her name. Finally, he glanced down at the tall black boy smiling at him at the back of the class.

"And of course Vernon, my campaign manager."

Ben gave a quick laugh and looked straight at Roberta.

"You see, I do know all your names already! Anyway, I just wanted to say that if you vote for me, I won't let you down. There are few things wrong with this class. There's a little too much bullying for my liking, and unlike some people, I don't think computer games are such a bad thing. I also think somebody should try to do something about those disgusting school dinners – long live Captain Codling!"

Everyone laughed and Vernon held his thumb up to Ben. He was doing just great!

"Seriously, I don't want to make a speech or silly promises like grown-up politicians. But I will say one final thing."

Ben looked round the class at his new friends.

"I'll do my best for you. That's all folks!"

And with that, Ben stepped down and returned to his seat. The whole class was silent. Vernon slapped his best mate on the back as he sat down.

"See, what did I say to you? Tell it like it is, Benny boy, and you'll do just fine. You wait and see."

"You'll all find a ballot sheet on your desks," Miss Calculate was explaining to the class. "Notice they aren't marked with your names. This is because voting is a very private affair. On the reverse side there are two boxes, one with Roberta's name and one with Ben's. All you have to do is tick the box of the person you want to see as your form prefect for the coming term. Put your hand up when you've finished and I'll come round to collect them. Tick away!"

With that, Miss Calculate turned her back on the class and returned to her own desk. Quick as a flash, Roberta jumped up on to her desk and held a placard aloft. "VOTE ROBERTA OR YULE BE SORY!" it said in large badly scrawled letters. Everyone recognised Robbie's handwriting, not to mention his atrocious spelling.

"She doesn't give up without a struggle, does she?" whispered Ben to Vernon.

Ten minutes later, it was all over. Just as Miss Calculate lifted the last ballot paper from Robbie's desk (he'd been puzzling over it for ages), the laser siren sounded the end of another school day.

"Class dismissed!" announced Miss Calculate. "I'll add these votes up tonight and tomorrow morning your new form prefect will be announced at assembly. Have a safe journey home, Pulsar Remove."

# CHAPTER EIGHTEEN

At Black Hole Primary's assembly the next morning – only the third one that Ben Gordon had ever attended – there was tension in the air.

Miss Wagstaff pushed the Head on to the stage as usual. This morning she was wearing a tangerine hot-pants suit in easy-stretch neoprene with lycra flame-coloured tights and matching tassels.

The rows of pupils sat down, cross-legged, on the rather chilly stainless steel floor. As they did so Ben turned round and caught sight of Roberta in the line behind him. She sneered at him, and stuck out her blue Martian tongue.

"Oi!" said Grudge, the odd-job robot, who was standing next to the sulky Mrs Danvers in front of a side door of the hall, "cut that out! Rude bloomin' kids."

Ben didn't remember seeing the likes of Grudge or Danvers in assembly before.

"Now, there's rather a lot to get through this morning," said Miss Wagstaff, "so listen carefully. First, the Head would like to say a few words."

There was the usual crackle: "GOOG MORNIL PUPIPS ... YESTERDAY'S CONCEL WAS SO SUCCESSY THAT, AFTER MUCH THOUGHT ... "

The Head's booming voice paused for a moment while his eye did an extra good swivel from left to right and back again.

"... AFTER MUCH THOUGHT I HAVE DECIDED NOT TO BUNISH COMPUTY GAMES. DON'T THANK ME FOR THIS, THANK BENJAMIN GORDIN IN PULSAR REMOVE - FOR HIS REMARKABUBBLE, EXPERTIP, PIANNIP PLAYING."

The children and staff burst into applause, and before the noise died down Ben whispered to Gracie who was sitting on the floor beside him: "And Ann Droid for some remarkabubble page turning!" They both tried not to giggle.

"Mega-result man!" said Vernon with a beaming smile, from Ben's other side.

"MISS CALCULATE WILL NOW DENOUNCE THE RESULPS OF HER FORM'S PREFECT DELECTIONS ... "

The Head's speaker went silent, and Miss Calculate stepped to the middle of the stage, a broad smile on her monitor screen.

"Thank you... Good morning everyone. As you know Pulsar Remove are in the middle of some very exciting elections to choose their form prefect. They handed in their voting slips to me as they came out of yesterday's concert, and I've now added them up – not very difficult for me."

There was a general stir of smiles and laughter at her little joke.

"And the result is most conclusive. Here it is: Ben Gordon (Independent Democratic Candidate): twenty-seven votes, Roberta Bar (Martian Domination Party): one vote. Ben Gordon is the new prefect."

The applause was even louder than it had been for Ben's Clayderhosen piano playing.

"She only got one vote, man!" said Vernon, shaking Ben by the hand. "And that would have been her own, so it means even Robbie didn't vote for her! Megatastic landslide, man!"

Roberta was looking around furiously at Ben.

"Quiet please..." interrupted Miss Wagstaff eventually. "I've got rather an important announcement concerning school lunches."

The very words "school lunches" brought silence to the room.

"As you all know, yesterday Mrs Danvers in the kitchen was unable to cook us lunch ..." lots of pupils smiled " ... and this was unfortunately because someone or other seems to have stolen her best saucepans."

Ben glanced towards Mrs Danvers at the other side of the hall. She had her arms folded across her large bosom and was looking angry. Her ugly chin stuck forwards like the bow of a very determined battleship.

"Now ..." continued Miss Wagstaff, "without saucepans Mrs Danvers has understandably decided that she cannot do her work and so the kitchens are closed. And don't all think that you're going to have fish and chips every day." A murmur of disappointment rippled through the room. "Unless whoever took the saucepans owns up, it will be packed lunches only at the Black Hole from now on."

"Oh, no!" whispered Vernon. "I can't stand my mum's packed lunches."

"Me neither," said Ben. "Last time she did one it was a lard sandwich and a ginormous mouldy orange."

"Well, that's better than anything Danvers ever cooked up," said Ann Droid, and the others had to agree that she was probably right.

"So there's one more chance," said Miss Wagstaff. "Will the person who took Mrs Danvers' precious saucepans please stand up now, and admit it."

Silence.

The staff, including the Head, looked

hard at the hall full of children. Ben realised that he felt guilty, even though it had nothing to do with him. He tried hard not to go slightly red, in case people thought it did.

"Very well then … " said Miss Wagstaff firmly. "Packed lunches from now on."

Suddenly there was an almighty clattering at the back of the hall. All the children swivelled round to see what was happening.

To their amazement the double doors at the back of the hall flew open, and in strode a huge man dressed in an immaculate Black Hole Patrol Warden's uniform. He had a red face with a horrible scar running down through one eyebrow and on to his cheek.

Behind him, to Ben's absolute horror, was Ben's mother. She was in her uniform too, but her arms were full of metal saucepans.

"OH NO!" said Ben under his breath. "Don't say my mum nicked the saucepans!"

"HEXCUSE ME 'EADTEACHER!!" bellowed the large man.

"ER…WHAT IS IT SARGEN MAJICK DAFT-VADER?" boomed the Head.

"HEXCUSE ME. But I believe that you was missing the school's saucepans."

"We are," said Miss Wagstaff, rather flustered.

"Well, may hexellent warden 'ere, Mrs Gordon, 'as apprehended them for you!"

"What?!" said Miss Wagstaff, amazed. "Please come up on the stage Sergeant Major."

The Sergeant Major and Mrs Gordon joined the school staff on the stage.

"Warden Gordon here," said the Sergeant Major indicating Ben's mum with his silver topped cane, "spotted the said saucepans being knocked off the Black Hole fence by one of your pupils. When she went to hinvestigate, they were floating in the direction of the Black 'Ole. Showin' total devotion to duty she dived over after them, and with great difficulty managed to prevent them bein' sucked forever into out darkness!"

The Sergeant Major stopped to draw breath. Ben couldn't take his eyes off his mother, as she stood there, arms full of pans, hat at an angle, looking embarrassed.

"SARGEN MAJICK, COD YOU IDONTIFY WHOCH PUPIP KOCKED OFF THE PINS?"

"Yes sah," Sergeant Major Daft-Vader

saluted. "It was that 'orrible looking 'erbert there, sah! That Martian with the mischief written all over 'er hugly mug. That's the one, ain't it, Mrs Gordon?"

Ben's mother nodded. It was Roberta all right. She'd seen it only too clearly.

"OND WHAT DO YOU SOGGIST I DO TO THIS WOCKED GEL?"

"Let me 'ave 'er for a couple of months, sah," barked the sergeant. "I'll soon knock the little madam into shape with square bashing, spud peeling and endless toilet duty. Oh, and while she's at it, she can learn to crochet too. Me wife needs some new coasters."

Slowly, the green blood drained from Roberta's face. In a trice she had collapsed into a heap on the floor. The thought of two months under the command of Sergeant Major Daft-Vader was too much for her to bear after the shock of losing the form election.

"OXCELLENT IDEA, SARGEN MAJICK, I LEAVE THE MOTTER ENTOREILY IN YOUR HENDS."

"Hang on, hang on!" shouted Mrs Danvers suddenly from the floor of the hall. "How did my pans get on to the Black Hole fence in the first place, that's what I'd like to know?!"

"AHH!" said Sergeant Major Daft-Vader, "I don't know that … But I do know one thing. THEY WAS FULL OF BRIGHTLY COLOURED PAINT!"

"SPEAK, MISTER GRUDGE!" said the Head's voice suddenly.

The children swivelled round again to look at Grudge. His face, normally a rather nasty nicotine-yellow colour, was turning pale. "I thought they was old tar pots," said the odd-job robot.

"OLD TAR POTS!?!" exclaimed Mrs Danvers beside him. "They're my best saucepans!"

"Well they had tar in them … " offered Mr Grudge.

"TAR!!! That's not TAR – THAT'S MY BEST SCHOOL CUSTARD!!!!" she screamed. "And I thought you was a GENT!"

"IT SEEMS," boomed the Head's voice, "THAT THE KITCHIP OPANS HAVE BEEN FOUNDED AND THAT MRS DANVERS WILL NOW BE ABLE TO COOK LUNCHINS. THANKS TO THE WONDERPIP ACTIONS OF

WARDEN GORDEN."

"Thanks a lot, Mum ... " said Ben Gordon as they all filed back out of the hall.

The rest of the children from Pulsar Remove gathered round Ben and slapped him on the back. "Great Mum!" Gracie shouted. "Cool lady," whispered Vernon in Ben's ear. "And she's pretty," said Hector. Ann took Ben's hand. "She's the best, Ben," the android announced.

"What are you all talking about?" asked Ben. "She's only gone and got us all school dinners back again."

"Yes," said Robbie, pushing his way through the throng and looking mightily relieved, "but at least she's given us all a two month break from Roberta!"

"Oh, yes," grinned Ben Gordon, new Form Prefect of Pulsar Remove, as he rushed to give his mum a hug. "I'd forgotten about that. Perhaps you're not such a bad Black Hole Patrol Warden after all, Mum!"